To Matthew, Kylie, Alice, Willem, John, and Oliver—M. B.

To Dad and Maxwell and other big softies—S. H.

Text copyright © 2000 by Margaret Beames
Illustrations copyright © 2000 by Sue Hitchcock

First published in New Zealand in 2000 by
Scholastic New Zealand Ltd., under the title *Oliver in the Garden*.

Library of Congress Cataloging-in-Publication Data available

ISBN 0-439-38576-8

10 9 8 7 6 5 4 3 2 1   03 04 05 06 07
Printed in Mexico 49 • Reinforced binding for library use • First
Scholastic printing, June 2003 • Illustrations are created on a Macintosh
using Photoshop 3.5 and Painter 5 • The text type was set in 21-point
Matrix Bold.

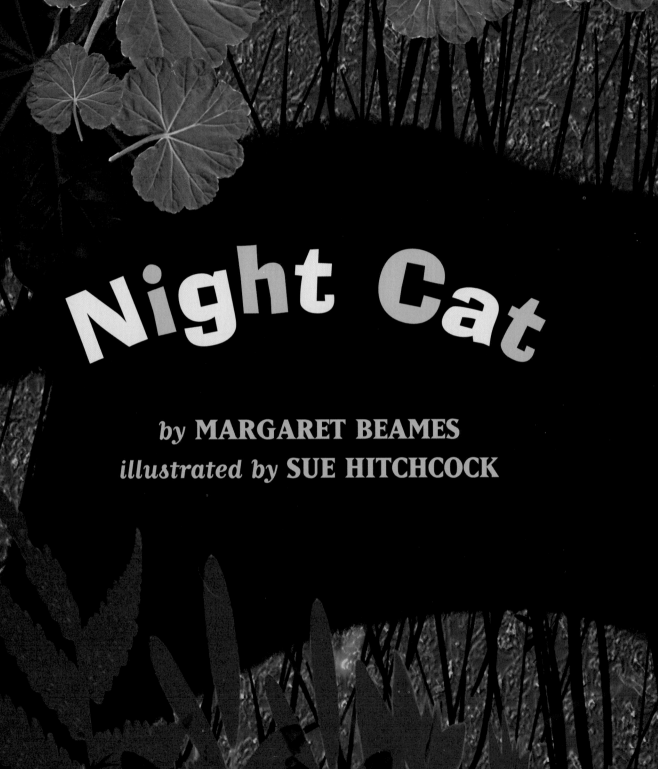

Night Cat

by **MARGARET BEAMES**
illustrated by **SUE HITCHCOCK**

Orchard Books • New York
An Imprint of Scholastic Inc.

The garden was full of light and shadows,
lamplight and moonlight—
full of things that danced and fluttered,
leaves and moths and trees.
It was exciting.

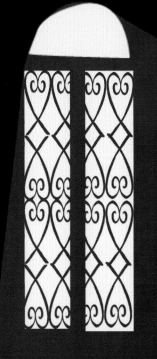

In the garden, Oliver said,
"I don't want to go to bed.
I want to stay out all night."

Mrs. Bundy opened the back door.
"Oliver!" she called. "Here, kitty!"

Oliver crouched low under the bushes.
He kept very still.

"Oh, stay out then, you naughty cat,"
grumbled Mrs. Bundy.
She shut the door.
But the light from the window
still shined in the garden.
Fat, furry moths beat against the glass,
trying to get to the light.

Oliver leaped up at them,
raking them down with his claws.
Crunch, crunch.
He gobbled them up.

Sometimes he bumped against the window.
Mrs. Bundy heard him and came to the
door again.
"Oliver? I know you're there.
Come along, it's bedtime," she called.

But Oliver was gone,
hiding behind the rain barrel.

"Oh, dear!" said Mrs Bundy.
"Then you'll just have to stay out all night.
I'm going to bed."
She shut the door and turned out all the lights.

Now the garden was dark.
Just the moon shined down on Oliver in the garden.
Now he could hunt and chase things all night long.

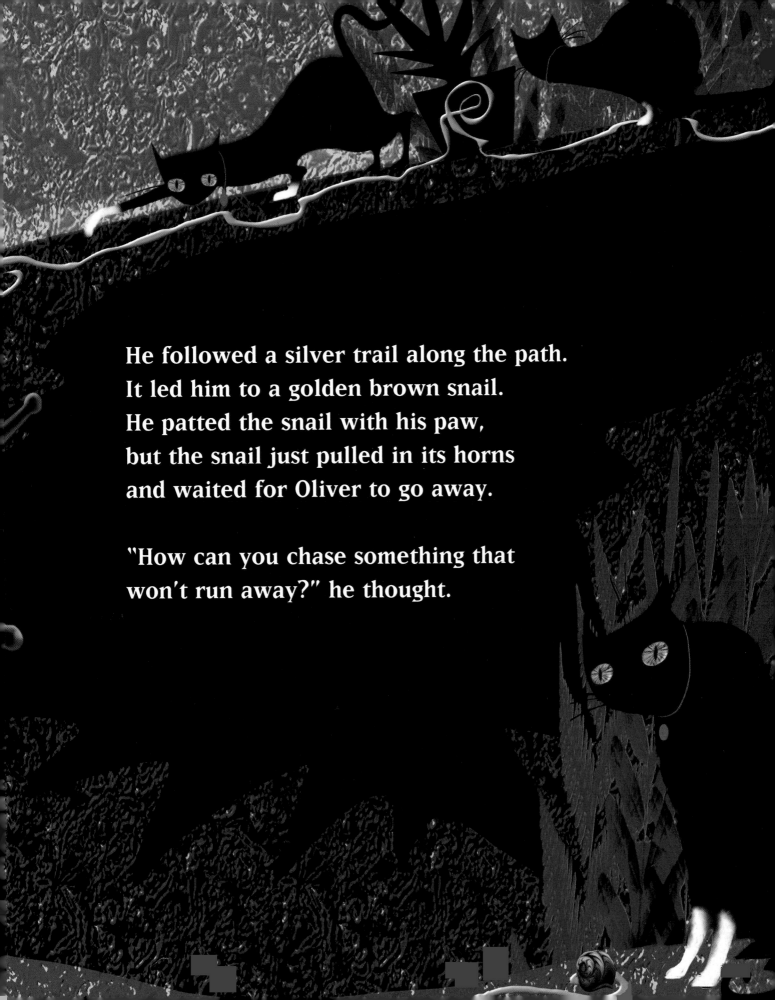

He followed a silver trail along the path.
It led him to a golden brown snail.
He patted the snail with his paw,
but the snail just pulled in its horns
and waited for Oliver to go away.

"How can you chase something that
won't run away?" he thought.

A porcupine stumbled and bumbled
across the lawn.
"That's more like it," thought Oliver.
He skittered after it, ready to pounce.
But the porcupine rolled itself into a ball
and waited for Oliver to go away.
"Ow!" said Oliver. "It's prickly!"

Oliver sat very still,
watching and listening.
A little gray mouse crept out from
under the garage.
It ran along the garden path.

Oliver's tail twitched.
His whiskers quivered.
His back legs wriggled, ready to pounce,
when down from the trees swooped . . .

something huge!

"Ye-ow!"

Oliver scooted to safety under the bushes.

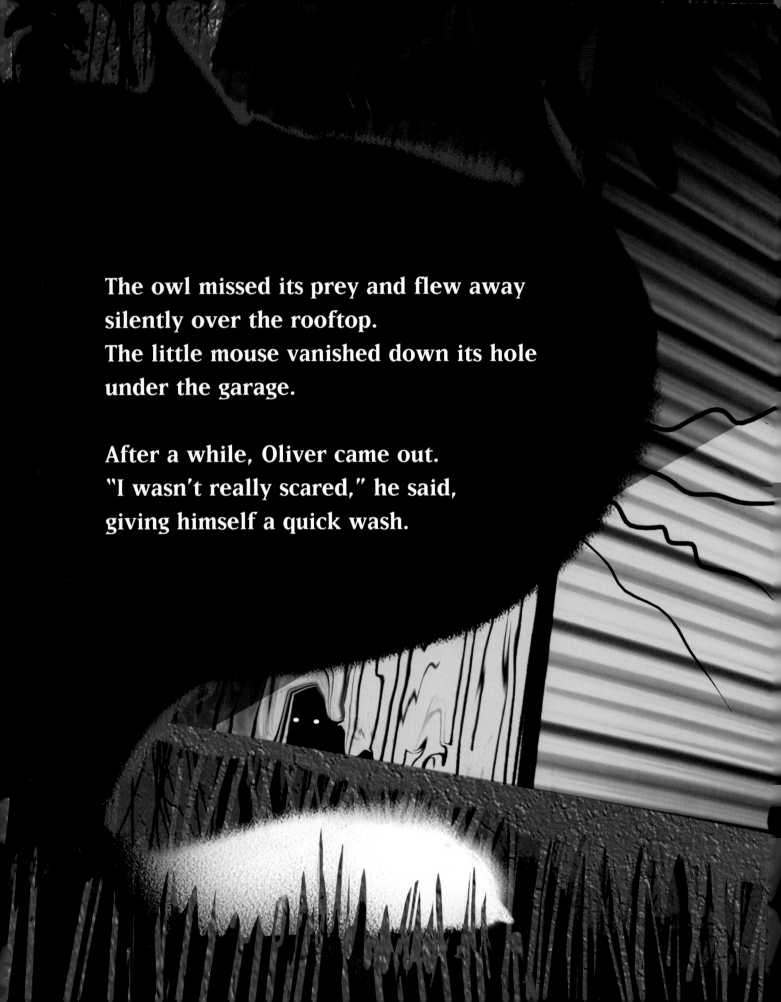

The owl missed its prey and flew away
silently over the rooftop.
The little mouse vanished down its hole
under the garage.

After a while, Oliver came out.
"I wasn't really scared," he said,
giving himself a quick wash.

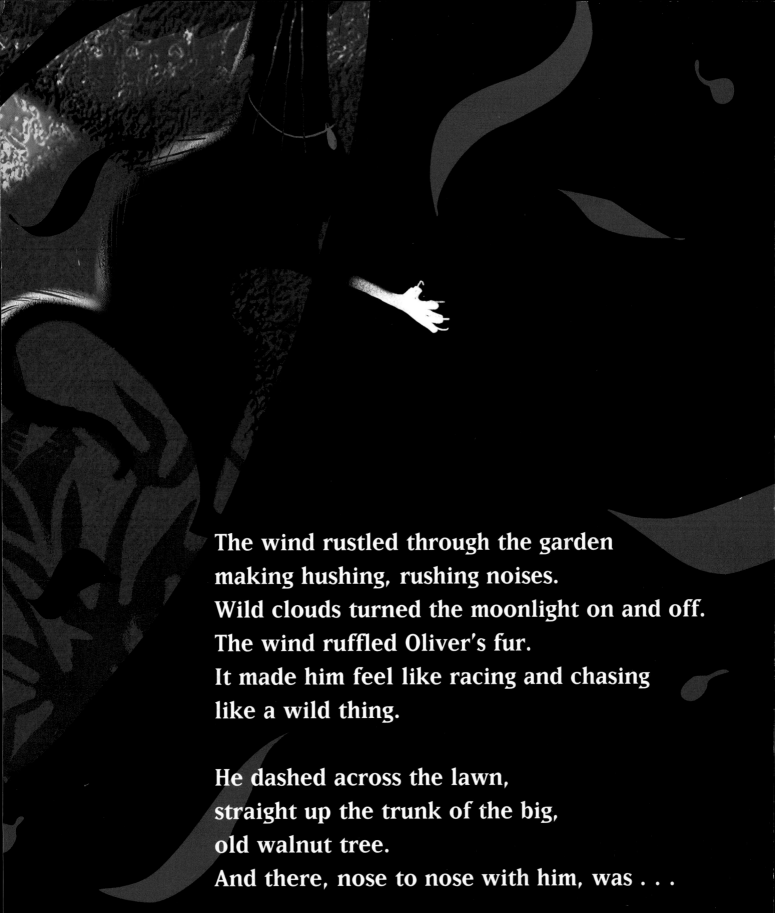

The wind rustled through the garden
making hushing, rushing noises.
Wild clouds turned the moonlight on and off.
The wind ruffled Oliver's fur.
It made him feel like racing and chasing
like a wild thing.

He dashed across the lawn,
straight up the trunk of the big,
old walnut tree.
And there, nose to nose with him, was . . .

a bright-eyed, furry opossum,
sitting in the fork of two branches.
It was bigger than Oliver!

Oliver backed down,
slowly,
then faster—and faster—and faster—
until he hit the ground, running.

Oliver wandered around the garden.
He wondered what to do.
The moths were gone.
Snails were boring.
Porcupines were prickly.
Mice were too quick,
and opossums too scary.

Plop!

A big, fat raindrop
landed on his nose.
Pit-pat, splitter-splatter,
more rain fell.

Oliver sat on the doorstep to keep dry.
He thought of his basket in the warm kitchen,
his cushion, and his saucer of milk.

He was tired.
The garden was dark and wet and lonely.

"I want to come in!" he yowled. "Me-ow! Let me in!"

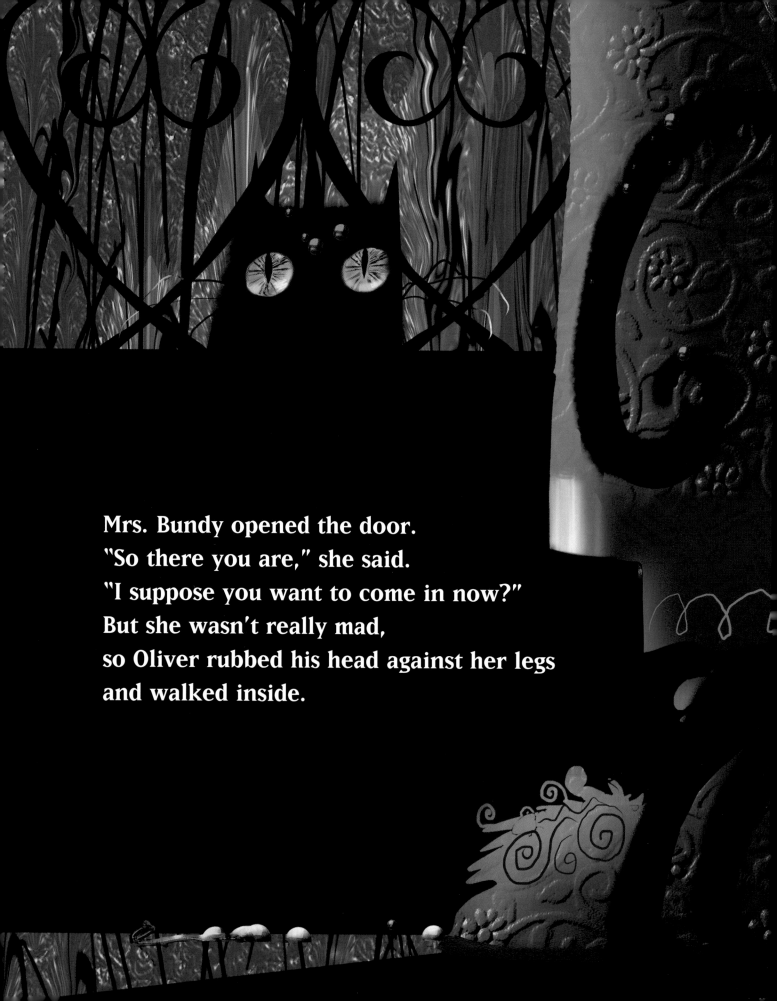

Mrs. Bundy opened the door.
"So there you are," she said.
"I suppose you want to come in now?"
But she wasn't really mad,
so Oliver rubbed his head against her legs
and walked inside.

He drank his milk and curled up
in his basket.
"I wasn't really scared," he thought,
"but she'd be lonely without me."